The Voice Around

1

Dedicated

To

Seidu Oluwafemi Olamide

And

Ajibade Iyanu Victoria

The Preface

The Voice Around is a collection of four short stories that are capitally labeled on politics and culture: two having debt to politics whereas the remaining two have debt to culture. The political part deals with how people can influence political processes and structures in a society through their voting powers and how politicians use political ideology to win the heart of the citizens through financial and secret-agreement instrumentality. The cultural part deals with how cultural activities are used to change the lifestyles of the contemporary children for better in a society and how children are given caution on how to be culturally oriented and obedience in order to avoid brutal punishment of ancestors.

Table of Contents

Royal Influence

It is another election period. Politicians of all levels both in the ruling and opposition party set decisive movements to royal fathers that govern populous cities in order to demand votes of the areas. Politics bring people together when she needs and disorganize togetherness when she equally needs. This regards politics as older than the players. In politics fate of losing and victory is centralized for no one knows where the favour will land as plenty people with different thoughts, grace and power are involved. In addition, betrayal is one of it paramount components. In politics, the fact that your opponent has visited a controller of a given kingdom for vote doesn't set room of discouragement to avoid attempting for your favour. Following this, royal father Ignatius received august visitors which are the powerful politicians of the ruling party on the account of demanding favour of vote from the territory.

The scene traced their appearance right from entering the palace compound till they come to the sitting point of the royal father. Exchange of pleasantries was observed. It is now time to unveil reasons behind the unnoticed visitation.

Honourable Johnson, the representative of the constituency remitted this: I and my colleagues present here and those that their present are not visible do register great deal of appreciation in regards to the favoring attention benefited by the party and our government from you. Words are irresponsible enough to express itself in an interest of offering you, but, do take our honour and respect for you and the great plan we have for the kingdom as the reference point. Though politicians are generally known to be a good player of words but consider ours beyond that. Our party policy is so much concerned about attending to all present and documented promises in order to have courage of revisiting and visiting our electorate without fear of anything. No one is perfect especially anyone who has public load or assignment. What can make them go astray is numerous. If my messager is good, you can attest to my kindness to the community. Giving and collecting is a law in human transactions; it is not hibernated with any form of favoritism. So, love should be parameter in nature. To prevent the time from losing it value, we are here again to demand for the usual favour. Our plans for the community have increased this time around by His grace there shall come alive as soon as possible upon reclaiming the seat.

The royal father submitted this: I hear you so clearly. Your composure is much matured. A public master or servant should be familiar with recommendations and criticisms. Their lives might not necessarily need and to the best rather it should keep path with better and good, for only the God meet the standard of all. Even as that, some are putting crash to that. I just quickly presented the above so as to keep you courageous on the subject of neutrality upon the service delivery. A good father must encourage the weak to be strong, the strong to be careful and to do the work for those who are neither weak nor strong. The failure of the leaders lies in their very hands and so as their success is, as respectively. The oversight knowledge on the service rendered so far is apprehensive. Power to do more is the grace we must certainly ask for. The success of knowledge and learning is questioning. For this, I will love you or any of your colleagues to help attempting my following questions: firstly, why do you count my throne so important and capable enough to help your party? Secondly, if I should campaign for one party and leave other people with their party, how can I be defined? Thirdly, how can I safeguard my community if others I don't support win? Lastly, how can I know the minds of my people before directing or encouraging them to support a party? Plenty questions are still alive but I should burry them for the sake of time.

Honourable Johnson responses: the first question may attract this answer: your peaceful pilot of the community has given opportunity of togetherness to the community. A well-structured kingdom is a good candidate for divine direction whenever there is a movement. Believing a leader of a kingdom upon extending hands of help is never a useless business as the impact of the throne can immediately offer favour or subsequent favour to your concern. You are a powerful man because you can handle situations without violence. The throne is important because it has a voice and a collective voice for that matter. Any throne that is community-oriented is an important throne for all has a say and chance of contributing. Secondly, a man or a human must die for one thing. Panicking of being known on particular stand is a dangerous move of a leader. Favour is seasonal as time do. Whosoever hunts for favour all times hunt for agony. Happiness and sadness is the artificial composition of knowledge. A man without public definition is an unfortunate being. For the sake of efforts, profit and lost is established. The fear of being known by a thing is a fear of tangible destruction. Human is authoritative and for that, encouragement to stand firm to defend yourself on what you love should be establish. Result of an action is not more than positive or negative. Human is familiar with the both. So anyone appear can be decisively dealt with. In addition, by hanging to a particular political party will set up a study platform for as many parties needing subsequent help to learn from the lifestyle of the supporting party as it is only an essential group you will ever live for following the rigorous assessment conducted to rank your throne. Thirdly, each community is an independent if the central power is highly constitutional and good. Human by choice is political defender and individual defense against external odds. No power is stipulated to underscore against communities that were supported by the losing party. For all communities are to be treated equal. If a representative of a particular society is good, there is no reason why the community will observe danger of making collective choice. Not all will support your political view due to right of self-governance and choice. So there is no fear in making up party interest. Finally, no one knows the minds of all his followers. Humans are the author of their choice. The greatest robbery and harm ever is to singlehandedly change human choice by personal interest.

The royal father interrupted good and good. Save the energy and knowledge for the next time. A good leader must teach his people what he knows and ask for what he does not know. Human brain is not water, for only water has all content within. I do appreciate your politeness and I equally enjoin you to set more records, upon your plan of developing the community. My people are highly literate. We have educated or learned people in almost all families of the community. And that will give me huge assurance that better people will be honoured. I haven't learnt to keep my stand concreted without defense. I will therefore say un-behalf of my people that we know better thing to do as long as we can all see. I can't waste your time any more. So, you are now free. Extend my warm greetings to your family and the other concerned people.

The stage kept alive till they met their entourage in the compound before they left the palace's compound. The security personnel ordered the gateman to reopen the gate two minutes after Honourable Johnson and his people left to their various places from the palace.

Here again, it is the set of the opposition party. They are here on the subject touched by their counterpart in the ruling party. What next? The stage continues with them from the compound to the royal palace's palour where they met and exchange usual pleasantries with the royal father.

Honourable Joel submitted this: we faithfully and honorably present warm regards to your throne. We have plenty communities under this constituency and in the full percentage of concern, we proudly give 70 percentage to the community for the uniformity of voice in supporting interested party. This has made the community a victory map of supported party. The non-violence election and collective support recorded from the community in the past years has earmarked the community as the strong-hold voting center of the constituency. I hope with collective voice as displayed from time immemorial, if put to test in the coming election, we shall gain victory definitely. Politics is for the old as it deserves patience and only the matured people like you organize victory for positions. So you are well deserved for our accolades. That is why we pick great courage to come over. We do know how you are a great campaigner of peace and development. Therefore support is mostly needed from you. If we are to be wholistically accessed by our doings, hardly is it to put some trust and believe against one another. I simply pointed this out to create window into helping one another on the positive reference account. We have better plans for the community. If you duly check, you can testify with me that, the strong collective effort the community plays during election for candidate of the choice is the reason behind the divergent development and growth of the community. This surely shows that you are a responsible king and forever our party shall continue to honour receipts of help extended for our victories in all levels. Once more we greet you and seek your effort to make our party win the coming election, your highness.

Royal father Ignatius responded: surely we live to support the good people and work. We don't know party rather we know candidates. Only the politicians should know their various parties. Our support only speaks for the responsible people or candidates. Therefore, only promise I do have is to use my power to compel my councils and people to collectively support the candidates with better records. I usually tell all politicians that come to me that only when my interest can be bought is at the mercy of the past good records of their candidacies as posterity will never forgive me if I should embrace my people to admire the wrong candidates for personal reasons. I therefore at this juncture assure you of our support if the candidate is found interesting. One man with good though can change his colleagues if only he is hugely determined and this is where our philosophy of interest is tagged, as respectively. I have equally received your opponent few minutes ago. But my council of elders needed to cross-examine all the candidates in their respective political parties before taking their various families as a campaigner. This will now keep your attention alive if your candidates are checked with great points. That is all. You can now go further in discharging your campaigns and un-behalf of my good people, I wish good-luck.

As the custom of the royal father Ignatius demanded, every time such visitation is honoured, he would later invite the council of elders which are the experienced and knowledgeable among others in the society to come over in doing examination of the respective political candidates in their various political parties. The elders gathered and the royal father, after exchange of pleasantries submitted this: my noble elders, our collective voice for positive things is ever increasing values of our efforts and knowledge about political circle and this has attracted much honour to our personalities that all the stronger political parties and the strongest in the time are seeking for our support. We should be very happy with that. For this, this very afternoon, I received the appearance and honour of the two leading political parties' members on account of submitting their will for our support in the coming election. As usual, I need to play a neutral role by identifying my desire to support the good candidates. Each of them came with a bag full of money. This is the reason why I sent my messager to you for the urgent meeting. I collected the money as the money is for community. I can't take the money neither I can't allow the money to be distributed among us rather to be used on projects that the community need. That is why I accepted the money and Chief Jonah was with me when they arrived simultaneously. All the money they share is for the communities. So if they can't use it to do development directly, we can collect it if we are been offered so that we can use it for the development on our own. Therefore, I have the following questions below to standardize the meeting: what are your takes in the coming election, which party can we uphold to, and paradventure the party we unanimously support fails to win, what can we do?

Chief Prof. Jacob submitted the answers: we are very proud of you. I think the words you gave them concerning your state of interest on the coming election as briefed me by Chief Jonah; you have duly and completely defended the community and your personality. Whosoever stand for a position equally stand to win or lose. The two are the only result expected in glamouring for position. All the prospective candidates in their various positions and parties are well known. I do know that before now, they might have visited some of us secretly to announce their desires. And as we do, we have checked their various records and we now know whom to choose among all. As we have one voice, the elders will secretly write their concerns on those candidates and get it submitted to the royal father while the royal father will then pick the candidates that have better points to their counterparts for endorsement. We shall then support the candidates with our various families. The royal father will keep such letters in the "Community Secretive Room" for retrieval if cases might arise on that subsequently. Note that the family or the community stands at a safer place either the unanimously supported candidates are not emerged. Equally note that, if there is no bias, the supported candidates need to win as other people will only use the pattern to checking records we do use. The reason the secret letter should be submitted on the account of candidates is simply for someone to equally use his family members to access such candidates because some of our wives and children do know about them as well.

The colleagues unanimously supported his move and answers by voting while the royal father ended the meeting with some few words which are: I am so ever happy to have all of you my council of elders. I often regard you as the council of wise. All issues are treated with maturity and understanding. The level of cooperation is beyond measure. And that is the reason behind our glory that attracts people to us. And I do enjoin the noble council to continue in the range so that we can surely live for one another. As stated by Chief Prof. Jacob concerning the voting of choice in the council concerning our political secret pursuit, I have all eyes on the road and the necessitated shall be done as soon as it is totally and collectively received. Let us do as we have been doing, as respectively. Once more, I thank you all and give my warm regards to your family as I close the meeting.

16

A meritorious stage opens to two great political gladiators of the ruling party of the state. It is a highly secretive meeting that commands the absence of their bodyguard from their immediate sitting positions. The setting of the meeting is applauded with light atmosphere. Dr. Jackson, who is regarded among the strongest and intelligent politicians of the very state and Senator John, who is also regarded as one of the political giant and player, both have their presence in order to put a record of discussion over the overwhelming flow of inner political game by their party chairman in the central and in the state. The both are still active in politics with powerful positions. But the state of their strong-hands in giving to the necessary ones in the party to earn total free, easy and quick endorsement against subsequent mandates is not recorded and thereby causing lapses over their ticket in the forthcoming election.

Senator John: my noble and ever supportive colleagues in the realm of powerful platform, the meeting aid at easing the designed loads placed over the success of our prospective positional ambitions in the nearest election. The high record of political concern labeled over our personalities most not be betrayed by all means. Politics is meant for the high-risker in all ramifications that have power to speak life to desirable manifestation. We have taken much by politics, politics have taken much from us, and so as, with us, politics can die and in politics, we can die. So, as we have power over her so as she has power over us. Taking good remember on the previous stakeholders meeting, we have literary lost party back-up over our prospective political ambitions.

We are no longer kids in politics and that will definitely offer advantage of plain understanding towards their lustful interest for our victory. The party chairman, with his overall power wants to make sure we are rendered useless towards keeping the mandates following his desire to offer punishment against our sluggish financial gift to his table. Now that the party chairman has indicted readiness to disgrace our political ambitions, what are best to be done to keep us alive in the ruling-corridor? To me, changing the party might be credited, because, it is better to lost seat in a new party than in the already mastered party. Excuses might attract listening if such dubious incident occur in a new party than the in the mastered party.

Dr. Jackson: you have spoken well. Nevertheless, some considerations need to be attended to save us from complete political destructions and rigmaroles. The major element or phenomenon we must hold to successfully design actions and reaction towards the present mess is intelligent. Politics betray or party betrays as many that betray her and so as an individual can betray as many party that betray him or her. In this sense, we must encourage ourselves to meet the political godfather of the party to hear final decision on the matter, because, the only person that can give exact account of secret deliberations and final opinions or plans without fear of anything is the political godfather of the party. In addition, if we can equally develop courage of meeting the party chairman for secret agreements, it can still gain usefulness. Moreover, definitely one among us can leave the party as I can't really predict if our tow ambitions are given favour, rather, I can perceive one among. But the final conclusion shall receive action as soon as the godfather gets to unveil all things to us. If we are to meet the godfather, it should be in the morning when the place will lack congestion of sophisticated level. I think doing this might be better to as earlier pointed out by you? No matter what happen, our relevancies must be secured by all means. Plenty options are on ground to be honoured if it seems all these are not giving better promising.

Senator John: I should accredit the presented opinions. If necessarily one among us should be honoured, collective support for one another to secure the ambition in the party or any party that might see our appearance must be kept alive, by all means. Paying visit to the party chairman is not a better ideal. Mind me that, Comrade Noah, the party chairman is very strong-hearted and highly keeping record on betrayer. So meeting him on this very matter is equal to not visiting as nothing can change his mind except money. And giving him money will certainly can't erase his dirty mind on us. However, do you think other way what others might have done to enable us see his bad reaction to us? Meeting the godfather, I follow you to buy the idea. He is an honest man and he does not take negative side except there are some positive orderings.

Dr. Jackson: thank you so much for the quick understanding. It is the strong-hood of our keepings. Together, we shall continue to be headlines on the political corridors. Better years is better future and better days is only for the continuous discharger of efforts with diligent and patience. Though, in politics, patience is not highly regarded. The strong people don't normally count the myths of patience in politics. Politics is a game and whatsoever game is the high key must not label trust on patience as the strong ones take advantages of all times. Nevertheless, the level we have attained in the profession can't give free hand to our total downfall in the pursuit. All times, whatsoever happens in politics is neither consider completely bad or good; simply, politics is for all, the citizens and the resources are the politics itself, whereas, the politicians are the opportune citizens to trade on less politically opportune and the resources of a nation. So politics is a game meant for all. Whatever is meant for all deserve thorough race to gain dominance as all are looking unto it. Though, politics don't demand strong-hand at the beginning. As you go deeper, you develop deeper ambitions and hearts and the host alike on it. Some take the game as a bigger race. But as you channel it, so it will appears. If you take it roughly, it will equally take you roughly and if you go smoothly, it equally goes smoothly. Let me just keep away the lecture. All of us know what it is. This very time, Comrade Noah will get to know that power is for all that are in the compound and not for only person in a compound. Let see what will happen. So let us see the godfather tomorrow morning to know the latest as we shall met tomorrow evening for the final conclusion upon the words of the godfather. Thank you so plenty. We are ever together and collectively, our political relevance shall be maintained.

Senator John: no problem. I shall text you where to meet by tomorrow evening after our successful visit to the party godfather early hours of tomorrow. Thanks.

They left the place to their various destinations upon agreeing to collective voice.

A stage opens to Justice Justin, the party godfather, the first-son of the party founder who left his law profession to join politics after the death of his father following a fact that no one is earmarked as a faithful politician to pilot the affair of the party fairly and transparently due to the over-sounding measure of bribery and corruption in the party and having a powerful ground behind the party deflation of original contents and attractions. Justice Justin has transformed the party very soundable from the initial level of it deploration after the death of his father, though he never developed an ambition for any political position or involving in politics, but keeping arms close to see the total destruction of the party his father struggled very well before the name attracts the public, having his life sacrificed for the party and having seen the party producing some influential men and women, he joined politics and do enormously excellent in all positions handled before attaining the party positon of godfathering.

Senator John and Dr. Jackson are around following their previous collective agreement to easily identify their space towards the coming election.

Exchange of pleasantries was duly observed and Senator John submitted this to mark the aim of their visit: your eminence, we are so glad and ever acknowledging the manners applied towards making the progress of the party. Though, hardly the record and regard of a founder is compared to another person or an ordinary member who has made some great contributions to the founded products. The value of the contributor is achieved on the joy of the owner. Truly, you have taken the steps of your father. God makes some of us great and successful through your father. The life of genius are always fruitful either they attain plenty years or not in life. The profession you left to join this end-time profession is very suitable for your kind and the position or title gathered from there is perfectly match with the current title in the party. All these now encourage us to come over to seek your final advice and contributions towards our different ambitions on the coming election. This is my submission.

Justice Justin: you are highly welcome. I must think that both of you are here for singular enquiry and purpose? Well, for coming over, I must be grateful. It is a good choice to come over to hear what has prompted the doubt in taking along with the coming election. Firstly, respect is given accordance to the works and worth of a person and for this, Dr. Jackson will receive my higher respect. I don't hate anyone. I respect all of you. I think most of you have taken higher years on earth to me, the opportunity of being born to rich family with intelligent channel of activities and the value of my father give reasons to the position I gained or do gain in life. I have learnt to grow age with knowledge. My father was a serious advocate on this very thought. He does tell me how to stay among the intelligent and the foolish, gentle and smart people as well as good and bad people. This is the particles of life. No one ever lived without making transactions with any of the above. If you can see very clearly, my former profession and the present profession are arenas that embrace all types of human beings and I can boldly say that those lessons have seen my source of survival. Let me narrow down the way, I only give approval. The decisions are made by the party executives and other valuable members. My duty is to give signature to the endorsed candidate or mandate and to help campaign for. It is gathered from the party that, Dr. Jackson is more submissive, transparent and accountable than you. The party is coming out from the recession. The party almost lost the values during the four years of my father's death when late Engineer Job was the godfather of the party. So the party presently needs honest people to boast the former glory. I have no say in the decision rather the approval in order to keep the safety of my position and the position of such deliberations. No one is against you. Only the party guidelines are against you and therefore the party want you to learn during the next tenure to see necessary reasons to be good in your in your position to the party and the electorates next you emerge winner in your ambition. Nevertheless, central compensations are available for you. I do promise that. Dr. Jackson, you are reserved for your political ambition whereas, Senator John will be given appointment that will teach him how to be more submissive the laws of the party and the minds of the electorate as usual. There should be no cause for alarms. Senator John, I will love to put your mind from dumping the party as the party still needs your type to strengthen her glory. If you can use this time to learn how to pay visit to your party members to know the latest and to pay attention to electorates to know and meet up their needs, this must be highly profitable and fruitful. There are necessities to live for your people. Remembering the source with goodies give expressway to progress and value of humans, therefore, not that, politics is for all. I will love you to see to this on plain and understandable directions to avoid mistakes of the future, as respectively. And to you, Dr. Jackson, you are to use the medium to do better, please. And paramountly, make sure your friend learn from that. Finally, Senator John, I will like you to be my friend. I like some of your natures. I think I have answered to your demands.

Senator John: thank you very plenty for the acknowledgement. I will definitely see how to do to that as soon as possible. I remain loyal.

Dr. Jackson: I am highly grateful for the concern and together, we shall push to the expected end. We are now taking our leaves and till we see in the next party meeting. Extend our love to the family.

They left there to their various destinations.

A stage once more opened to the seating points of Senator John and Dr. Jackson when it is darker to as the same time of their meeting in the previous day at another place. This time, final deliberation will be registered to see how their positional personalities are not completely erased following the inner fight in their political party.

Senator John: we thank ourselves once more for coming. I hope if you have taken deeper thought on the words of Justice Justin, having known how stubborn I am, it is better for them to come up with such as early as this as they do know how I can harm that party if they try to betray me at the last point. But, seeing how merciful you are, you are kept to be betrayed at the last point where no political party no longer change their candidate for the influential people coming. So, must you wait to be disappointed at the last days? I suggest it is better we move together. It is none stopping journey for me but I don't know of you.

Dr. Jackson: yes. I am not holding you back. The best we should do is to keep an agreement with each other. Though there is no trust in political circle. But that doesn't stop trusting. So, in order not to be kept away from political relevance, we must be intelligent and patience enough to embrace little maturity and understanding in taking the final decision, as customary. We must therefore not put our legs in one basket. The world betrays but not in all angles at the same time. You can defect to another party while I remain in the party. We shall offer secret support to one another so that, if you win and I might be betrayed, you can help my relevance, so as, if you are betrayed over there, I will help your political relevance, as customary. Going from the party the same time might build total destruction of our political career. Because, even the new party must lost hope of doing things with us as the label of betray is seen in our personalities. One thing we must equally know is that, nothing is permanent. No one is wiser than the activities because mistakes are seen after the actions. We have acquired much and even if we lose this coming election, subsequent elections are awaiting for our success if we do not give up as usual. So don't worry at all.

Senator John: thank you so much. I don't accept the words of others but I do respect your words as you always talk senses. We shall do as said and agreed upon. By tomorrow, I will visit opposition party in their meetings as my deflection will be announced tomorrow evening or afternoon on the television stations. As the country inter-party system demands, we can only talk on phone from now till the election is conducted. Defecting so that we can continue our normal activities and lifestyles might be seen after the victories. Together and forever, we shall be therefore one another.

Dr. Jackson: no problem. Give my love to the family and do caution your wife on this so that her movement should not create enormities against the move and her hide out with my wife must be put to stop for this period. In addition, try to be careful over there. Goodnight the brotherhood.

They left to their various destinations.

The following day, Senator John was received to the opposition party after some deliberations by the party executives. The area of deliberation is on the betrayer they might experience from Senator John after he emerged winner on the party platform. Different points were measured but finally, he was accepted as no one knows the heart of humans and that betrayer can come from any person and anytime and that betraying is a familiar concept in political party.

The election was conducted and by the inter-party secret game that was played by Senator John and Dr. Jackson, both of them won their similar positions with the different platform.

After the election, they met and talked on the necessities to be in the same party. Plenty measures were put in place and the both agreed and joined the party where Dr. Jackson is in order for continuity as lesson is learnt already.

Royal Agony

28

Royal father Justin is a respectable king in his kingdom. His wisdom has generated a lot of advancements in the major areas of the kingdom. His joy ever is to see all having colourful life and his greatest dedication is allocated to solving solutions of his people carefully with peace. He tackles issues with profound leverages and levity. His desire is overwhelmed upon making good command the best which is better in humanity is what he seek for all and for that, he put a lot of efforts and contributions to as many that glamouring for good things. Despite his high level of understanding and knowledge, never once has he discriminated anyone. This makes him the king of all. Meeting the desire of the youth in the kingdom is the better channel of establishing peace and growth in the society and this makes him weekly have meeting with his youths. He advices the youths and enjoined them always to submit their hidden burden so as to see how to collectively attend to them or that. Saying that the real safety of a community is established in the standard choice of the youths. Youths have capacity to easily organize and disorganize crisis or growth. This encourages him to be nearer to the youths in order to see how to command positive lives in them. Where is the joy of throne aside having obedience youth? How can this be fully established? It can be done with simplicity. Youths are to be taught with humor, because, adult education is one of the hardest job in life as high percentage of patience, carefulness and understanding are the major agents that are capable of commanding conducive environment for such learning. The divergent and different characters possessed by the youths, at times create long-term gab for assimilation and acceptance of any given idea; this open knowledge of interactive session to the royal father as he uses the medium to hear the views and opinions of all.

A kingdom is a total collection of all types of human in humanity. Each kingdom is powerful enough to create all types of humans. Taking study from the youths of the generation, it is highly comprehensive that, gab in similar knowledge and understanding definitely take a larger scale. Some youth go out of the kingdom to hunt for foreign lifestyles and onceexhibited with mastery or not, they take joy in coming back for such promotion. This is one of the strongest medium we have a divided kingdom. Even as this happens in the kingdom, royal father Justin usually gathers such group of youths for special counseling of life. Some hear to decrease antagonistic lifestyles whereas others hear to increase the level of their porous activities in the kingdom to have dominance in such given area. This has enabled different philosophies in a kingdom. Some are capable to influence others whereas some are not. Nevertheless, each touches community. This definitely makes a community a strong-hood of difficulties.

The joy of the royal father is equally established on a fact that his council of elders has similar philosophy and urge for the betterment of the youths and the kingdom at large. This makes them devote some of their precious time attending to matters that can help the youths have rich knowledge about life and good for the only safety of a community comes from the youths. The youths are capable enough to invite internal and external crisis that can completely destroy a community. The fruitfulness of the efforts make the community has two set of youths, the better-minded ones and the wrong-hearted ones. The joy of the effort is registered upon having higher numbers of youth with better minds. So the antagonistic activities are easily curbed and the rebirth or birth of porous activities receives hard labour and sometimes lost effort of delivery. This is what is on point.

One good afternoon, Jackson, the only son and the child of royal father Justin returned to the community for town. He is a young tall handsome guy and necessarily the next king. The royal father should be happy but latter days would bring hard days for the king over the strange and bad characters of his son. What is happening? The married characters will soon put him and his group in bitter trouble in the village.

As he come to his father, sincere greetings from me to your royal-hood. I am happy to be at home and I think it is a better place for me so far. I say this earlier simply to distract you from demanding reasons behind my return without information and without the stipulated time as agreed. But you must know that changes accompany seconds in life. Agreement is not safe in the room of changes. So, I will not give you chance to tell me to go back. I have some stresses from the movement so I therefore demand to go and rest.

The royal father responded: you are highly welcome my son. We are happy to see you particularly your mother that want to be with you all times forgetting you are old enough to set some house-hood minds. For no reason a child should not be welcomed in his house but I must equally say that, whatsoever has reason in one particular place might not has reason on the other place. I must keep you rested for a while as I think we have this evening to talk better. Once more you are welcome.

Jackson left the area to his room after meeting his mother and as soon as he left his father sitting point to his room, Chief Dr. John arrived in the sitting point of the royal father. After exchanged of pleasantries, Chief Dr. John submitted this: your royal highness, I am here to offer thanks for the endurance put on a surface of my son's dubious acts. You have judged squarely in reference of better understanding. I do pray that may your son gain such wisdom. At times we talk things that make us get relieve from the danger of the hour of death. We have almost used our lives. We thank the gods for the divine guidance. The final job of every father or parent is to help the children go closer to where there should be in the society before death. Children are the representative and successor and that is why we must not lost courage in putting them on right paths before death. The kingdom is ever proud of our ruling. That is why I am praying to the gods to grant such wisdom to your heir. Though only what is thought can be graced to and for. So your major work now is to train your son on the light paths as you do enjoin.

Nevertheless, experience and knowledge gathered so far has taught us how and why the sons of the good-hearted ones do go astray to the foundation of their father. But I do sure Jackson will make a good character for you has done things that can give you happiness. I am telling you to be conscious of his movements in the community in order to be at a safer arena for the successful take over in the later good years. You have positively changed the lives of some of the previous notorious youths and with great assurance, it is established that your son will make a good life from your words. I am setting way towards the township hall for a meeting with some of the youths on the previous plans designed in the meeting. So do extend my warm love to the family as I am battling with time to meet up. Maybe, I will see Jackson when next I come around. I saw him while coming before I went to see Chief James.

Okay. They will hear that exactly. Do give my greetings to the youths and for losing time of agreement, I should no longer take pleasure in embracing that. So we can talk better later. Take care. The royal father said this.

It is in the evening after dinner. Royal father Justin sent for his son and his wife. As usual, they honour the invitation and the royal father had this submitted: I greet you my loves. Jackson you are my strength and your mother is my love. I call you my strength because you are the hope of the family and the community at large. Your mother is my love because he takes care of me all the times and she does what my daughters should have being doing. And I can therefore boldly say, I am nothing without you. So I have overwhelmed joy and happiness to have my strength and my love beside me now. If I should die now, I have better chance to win big seat over there. To you my son, I once again highly welcome you. The gods would have a better chance to punish me if I ever have a hidden agenda or reasons behind my little or less support to see you around the village this very moment. As agreed upon, it is better you come around when I am nearer to the ancestors by theways such is detected or whenever I demanded your appearance for some ritual cases or otherwise. But I can now say it is to my surprise to see you unexpectedly. The worst is a pointer to the less concern to put us on the same knowledge of your movement. Though you are matured enough to undertake some things without our notice, but, I am also letting you get knowledge that it is irresponsible to do things out of genuine reasons. If your attention is needed, I should be the one to make request of your appearance. What you must know is that, to any area goodies are found, bad spirit stand standard to subdue such atmosphere. If the immortals have enemies how much more can the mortals have? Though one should not acknowledge them but I think it is in the school of idealism whereas in the school of realism, great attention should be allocated to that. Humans are spiritually-oriented and this makes possible chance to be vulnerable to plenteous spirits. Who knows the one that will gain prominence at the door of internal and external entrances? Think very far. It is my desire to have you around to teach you better about the culture, but, it is my joy and happiness to see you far away from the village now to keep you safer. I do know what I am telling about. I mean better things for you. So let me hear reasons behind this.

Jackson submitted this: though I don't really have genuine reason behind my coming. But, I feel to just come home now to learn some things and to have rest of mind. Father, it is as simple as that.

Royal father Johnson responded: I hear you. But I am not comfortable. This is your house and the throne is yours. So I can't say you should go back immediately. You can relax little but have mind of going back soon, please. And for the time you are to stay in the village, I will love you should leave in isolation for safety reasons. If you can learn how to walk alone, you are leaning how to make changes, but if you keep all your movements with others, you prepare yourself to get helped and not all help is suitable for someone like you, earnestly. Take note of that. You should know that our culture is highly disciplined. Our culture is surrounded with numerous boundaries. Punishment is fatal and final in our culture and there is no bias in all of these. The gods appear in all forms so you must therefore learn how to keep peace with all things. The gods are essentials in judgment and technical in changes. I do know before now that you are now familiar with the culture following the letters I do send to you concerning the culture? I must advise you candidly that the ways of the culture differs from all you have learnt from the university and the town. So keep a better watch to the culture as it is what you are born for and what you will definitely die for. My son, take all this words and you shall find peace in the land. Finally just note that all you have been indulged in from your previous areas should be dropped so as to keep emulation of the cultural life alive. I will be embarking on a journey for a brief meeting at the state headquarters tomorrow morning. I therefore wish to go to bed early to wake early for the movement. If we can't see before I go tomorrow morning, it should be in the afternoon I get to return.

Each left the palour to their various rooms.

Jackson being a popular guy before leaving the village for University studies before staying in the town for little period have some of his friends who are still ate the village welcomed during the movement of his father for a meeting. Though this father left earlier while in the later hours, his mother equally left to see one of her counterpart she wish to marry one of her daughter to her son. He set up the movement simply to notify her friend to come to her place with the lady she want for her son. So, it is during the period Jackson received them. They were around with their drinks and smokes and girls. The entertainment was so rough for the palace. The ancestors of the land being essential bodies used spiritual chains to arrest two elders' heart to visit the royal palace that very moment despite the knowledge of the royal father's movement is at their respective knowledge. They trekked to the royal palace and upon meeting them, rude reactions were held between them in a space to correct them, but, the boys refused totally to agree to the elders' opinions and impartations. So, angrily, the elders left there in order to come back later to honour the king's arrival and to mark the custom that, the council of elders must come to the palace to have meeting with the royal father in regards to his movement for the day. Even as that, the boys still continued till they were tired.

In the meeting as the royal father returned, after the royal father has briefed the elders on the movement, the two elders that witness that remitted this and cross-examination into the matter were on before the Chief Priest of the village arrived with the message: the gods directed me to the meeting to give you go ahead of punishing the boys squarely. The gods directed that the royal father should not be part of the judges and as many that their sons are involved in the defiling the royal palace. Therefore the oldest elder should judge the case and the punishment should be labelled upon all indulged and the greater portion should go to Jackson for not only accept the visitation of the worthless but for taking part in promoting their foolishness and finally for disobeying his father's words and arguably doing as wished. The gods equally warned against biases in making the case as they promise to punish all those that will like to wrongly defend for hidden agendas or purposes.

The Chief Priest disappeared and within some period of time, the case was voted and the punishment is announced for take up.

Here is the judgment and voting: the culture is known to be intolerance about any porous activities set up by any group of men or women, boys or ladies and the punishment is ever capital with unnegotiable nature as any bias employed in punishing offenders or offender must surely walk back to destroy the joy of the society. As documented in the law of the palace, such activities must attract punishment of exile and as we do not entertain cross-section and cross-examination which might open ways to bias of any type, I hereby sanction the players of the victim to 5 years exile as this will go on a long run to disassociate such manners from the land following the unanimous vote voted. Thank you all for the time and may the gods honour for their careful watch and clean judgment.

Stranger Crash

Justice and Julius are best friend. They are working class boys in town. The level of their friendship is so intimate that led Justice to take Julius to his village during two weeks of their yearly leave. The both are intelligent and stubborn. But the level of Julius state of stubbornness is lower to that of Justice. And for that a reason, Julius was so careful not to receive any bad record in Justice's village during the stay. This equally strengthen their friendship as Justice's parent solely approves their friendship seeing the level of compatibility in the both following the measures in their intelligence and care. In addition, both of them are handsome and they attended the same university and got similar job the same time with similar place.

It is a period of annual festival of Christmas and New Year. Justice follows Julius to the village for the celebrations. The family is so happy to see them. It is three days to the Christmas when they arrived. Julius' parent were not around when they arrived. So, after the dinner, Julius took Justice to his parent for necessary information about the boy and the parent. After taking the seats in their seating position, they greeted one another before Julius submitted this to his parent: my strengths and my love, here is Justice my good friend right from our university days. We are opportuned to secure similar job in the same company at the same time as well. I have examined his characters and I can boldly say he is good and that equally encouraged me to take him along for celebrations. And Justice, here is my parent, the only ones I live for. They are so amazing and good-cultured. God makes me to be whom I am today through them. So my high respect for them. So that is that and his father make response afterward.

Julius' father: my children, both of you are highly welcome. I am so much happy with your gift. Earnestly, these celebrations are for me. Justice, I can see a high rate of compatibility between you and Julius. So, I urge you to continue in the way. Make your friendship fruitful and valuable. And as both of you are together, I do embrace you to share the knowledge of your culture to one another. Culture is human identity and it is the components of humans. So the first thing to study about someone is the person's culture. A lot of mistakes are meant to be done. The present generation do not embrace that and that is why mysterious death is the order of days now. In our good time, that is how we do. But there are still areas where those life is still going on, as respectively. Nevertheless, my duty is to expose your knowledge to our culture as respectively. So I can tell you that we have the finest culture so far among our contemporaries following the peaceful, divine and holy nature the culture is structured on. The culture spans all over the activities of it citizens and most violoations attracts dreadful or death punishment. So it has made the villages more careful about their daily activities. Here are some cultural practices: no matter how an elder appears or known to be stupid, the younger ones are mandated to respect him or her like the parent, any child that refuses to respect his or her parent must be reported to council of elders and any decision made upon the child will be enforced, male child and female child of the same family are not given room to stay together over the night, no one should insult the other in a stream, a stranger must see the chief priest for protection before going to our river or stream, the heart of the villagers must be fair and free against others, any girl found interested must be taken to the parent before sexual intercourse, these and many others are available but I hope Julius will tell you the rest or I will tell you the rest tomorrow evening by the power of the gods. Don't panic. The village is very safe for you. I am very tired for the day. So I will love to go to bed now.

Justice: thank you so much for the enlightenment and I hope I will hold to it. Because, we equally have culture but it is not similar to yours. From the look of things, the village has better culture to as ours. No problem I have to honour yours as I am in the land. No one is wiser than the land nor has power of questioning the land for any reason. Justice and Julius need to go out to meet some of Julius' friends especially ladies whose after some years are only opportune to see during the yearly celebrations. So as they go out, they meet different types of ladies who are socially updated following the demonstration of characters. Justice no longer endure after seeing beautiful ladies within charting up with them and he told Julius his mind while Julius' gives go ahead to that as that becomes the normal life of the present era.

Now Gloria is sighted afar from their standing position and Julius has earmarked Justice for that and happily as they move down closer, meeting the standing point of Gloria, they waited little so that she can end the call before talking to her. After the call, Gloria greeted them and she submitted this to Julius: so you are now enjoining? Why can't you extend such atmosphere to me? I am now jealous of your girls. I know how you normally play rough on girls and that is why I refused to agree to your concern then and my friend who later agreed for you got total huge disappointment. Hope you have changed from that lifestyle? Nevertheless, I think you are moving around to check your ladies who stay in the village right? Don't give them all you have come with as I will definitely have share from it. So how are you doing and who is the guy with you and hope both of you are not using the period to terrorize the village ladies with your sweet tongues?

Julius: oh! I know how ladies have verbal diarrhea, but yours become abnormal all times. Why can't you buy respect for yourself in the sight of a stranger you know he is capable of taking a lady to house now? Nevertheless, I am doing very fine. I can equally see good changes in you. Definitely, your guys are taking proper care of you. Without taking much time as life is well scheduled, just try to have some time with my guy as I will love to visit one of my friends. You can take my friend to your house while I meet both of you together after I get to finish my visiting, please. I have changed. So don't be harsh on my friend. It is now time we plan deeper on taking a wife and husband. Therefore, let us not try to misuse any opportunity in such platform any longer. Hope your friend is fine and I do hope also that she is around for the celebrations? She loves this period. Thanks.

Gloria: no problem. She is fine and she told me she is on her way home for the celebrations. The tight schedule in her office is the reason behind her late movement for the day. I am equally fine by God's grace.

Julius: all right thanks. Now meet with my humble friend, Mr. Justice. The name should definitely enlighten you about him. His parent is intelligent like him so the name given is suitable. So just try to understand with him, please. Don't disappoint me, okay?

He began to move from their points gradually before Gloria replied that there will be no problem. Okay I will meet you there later. Thanks. Julius concluded that as he moves.

Justice: the young beautiful and promising lady, nice to meet you. How are you doing for the day?

Gloria: I am doing fine. Sorry do you mind following me to my house, because, it is no longer ideal we should stand on a road to honour our discussion with the level of age we have attained so far. In addition, our traditions respect any guy and lady that take themselves to any of the house, especially the female house for such talk. I know where you are heading to already. So, better we go to my house to aid better chance to talk lengthy as usual.

Justice: I highly find pleasures in that. This will equally safeguard our lives and personalities. So, let us make that possible my dear and thanks immeasurably for the kind gestures.

They move towards her house's direction as collectively agreed upon.

Now, they have settled down in a free space left with only two of them after Justice got to greet her parent and siblings around. Looking each other for a while, Justice opened the discussion.

Justice: beautiful Gloria, you do know the solid state of my mind now. We are matured enough to understand the lyrics and myths of love. Though plenty things might give rise to doubt in love but we should not that, love between humans is a risk in the present era as the original concepts of things are not honoured after the attention is gained. Ladies always have doubt of trust in live and the negative effects of disappointment are usually their inheritance and for this, most ladies of high intelligent found it difficult to accept a guy not known before. I must equally tell you that no one is truly known. The heart of humans is far from activities but nearer to determination and desire. So taking a whole year to study a guy is useless in my dictionary. What I believe is that, in live high opportunity is earned to study and put to taste your partner. No one is perfect and we are dedicated to divergent philosophy of life. Therefore, one should not put much regard to disappointment; rather, desire should be built on how to amend one another, as respectively. I am not trying to brainwash you any way. I love telling girls or ladies the truth of the era. Remember that either I get you or not, my life continues as usual. So there is no tangible reason for me to provide stories that can't matters simply to get advantage over you. I no longer have much to say. Therefore, let me hear you, the beautiful lady.

Gloria: you are spoken well. But, earnestly, guys should not be trusted and ladies as well in the present era. This has given difficulty in having a life partner now: husband or wife. Though, despite the fact the world is occupied with high numbers of betrayers, we still have some trustable people. Inter-ethnic marriage is allowed in our culture. You speak intelligently and maturedly. In addition, you are handsome. I am a lady that embraces self-trust and confidence. I believe no one can dare play successful antagonistic game and score totally free on me, for that, I will give you chance of trail as demanded. We are culturally active in the village due to some strange punishments that are endorsed by our ancestors all times. I hope Julius has enlightened you more about our culture? Even if Julius hasn't, I strongly believe that, his father has done so, because, his father is a highly traditional elder of the village and he is so much respected for that. In this village, higher respect is given to the doers and advocators of the traditions and not necessarily on the wealth or knowledge acquired by the contemporary's activities. So take note on those instructions to avoid building harm to yourself and to the family during your stay and as we go higher and further, I will tell you the part women involves to expose to their partner.

Justice: I am so happy for your concern and your response. You are indeed intelligent and studious. I therefore do promise to be a good man to you. Thank you so much.

Just exactly a minute from that moment, Julius' voice was heard from their sitting positions as he exchanges pleasantries with Gloria's parents and siblings. He was directed to their sitting positions by Gloria's father. Julius met them on promising moods. He was so excited as well seeing his friend getting a lady over there as that will give more consolidation to their friendship as usual. After little jokes by the both in the presence, Julius opens the discussion.

Julius: hope all of you have gained the purpose of the meeting as we must set on our ways. My daddy has been calling me to come home quickly so as to slaughter the goat he just bought for the celebrations as usual. So what is on ground Justice?

Justice: everything is okay. Gloria is so intelligent to know the importance of time and season. So I can now tell you that we are in love with one another.

The both laughs and Gloria was given taken for the celebrations by each of them and Gloria promise to give them food for the celebration the next day and they agreed also to see each other after around 1: PM the next day. They now left there for their destination.

It is on Christmas day, after Julius' parent and siblings have gone out to celebrate the day with some of their friends in the annual or yearly meeting; Justice and Julius are left in the house. Justice has taken birth and he is in a room robing cream before putting on the dress whereas Julius is in a bathroom, a young beautiful girl enters the room immediately with food, I am a sister to Gloria and she told me to bring this food for you, but she is a spirit, as soon as she kept the food on the table, she rushed and hold Justice manhood and immediately uncovers her dressings, Justice no longer control himself until he found himself untop of the lady. Within some minutes, the deed has been done and the lady left there. Julius was doing plenty things in the bathroom so this enable Justice got more time to dress up before he arrived. Justice pointed to the food as he told him that a younger sister to Gloria just brought the food. Ash! Have she forgotten the culture of the land that a lady who wants to marry a guy will bring any food prepared for her guy singlehandedly and eat such food together? This can see limit as soon as the bother get engaged. No problem. I will remind her when she comes as we can only eat the food whenever she comes. Julius said this and before Julius could dress up, Gloria arrived with the food. She entered the room after she was given order following her knock on the door. Justice and Julius were surprised at seeing her with food. Do you want to kill us with the foods? How can we finish up the foods? The one your younger sister brought is still intact so why are you adding more? Gloria responded: I haven't sent any of my sisters here. The tradition does not entertain that. Ash! It should be a testing spirit; I told Justice that it is very untraditional to do that. But I have gotten the matter now. No problem. Thanks to God that my father just arrived to take something as I am coming out of the bathroom. He will take the food to the chief priest for purifications. Let me see my father for this. As Julius set to see his father, Justice followed him outside and told him all that happened.

Both of them met Julius' father and told him all these.

The joy is that, such test form the gods attracts no punishment as the gods is aware of that to command promotion to the family and the boy and lady that host such reasons.

Julius father rushed to the chief priest and within some minutes, they arrived there. The both are inside Julius' room. The chief priest said the following before the purifications and spiritual engagement of Justice and Gloria: the gods are always gracious to their true advocators. The gods has visited the family with goodies. And as from today, the family members of all that are here will continue to enjoy the grace and fruitfulness and progress from the gods. Justice and Gloria are created for each other. The traditional requirements have been satisfied so anything can happen between them from now onward. I don't talk much because the gods don't talk much. Actions are the birth right of the gods while talks are for the mortals. Jonah, the father of the house, get to the royal father later to tell him this so as to be put into the royal palace record as the family is due to be selected as a king or queen in the later years. He used some minutes to purify all of them and the entire compound at large so that the spirit should not come back to take the goodies before he left.

www.ingramcontent.com/pod-product-compliance
Lightning Source LLC
Chambersburg PA
CBHW020515160726
47991CB00007B/2970